mary-kateandashley

Surprise, Surprise!

Look for these

titles:

mary-kateandashley
TWO of a kind ™

Surprise, Surprise!

by Megan Stine

from the series created by Robert Griffard &
Howard Adler

HarperCollins*Entertainment*
An Imprint of HarperCollins*Publishers*

A PARACHUTE PRESS BOOK

A PARACHUTE PRESS BOOK
Parachute Publishing, L.L.C.
156 Fifth Avenue
Suite 325
NEW YORK
NY 10010

First published in the USA by HarperEntertainment 2001
First published in Great Britain by HarperCollins*Entertainment* 2003
HarperCollins*Entertainment* is an imprint of HarperCollins*Publishers* Ltd,
77-85 Fulham Palace Road, Hammersmith, London W6 8JB

TWO OF A KIND characters, names and all related indicia are trademarks of
Warner Bros.™ & © 2000.
TWO OF A KIND books created and produced by
Parachute Publishing, LCC, in cooperation with Dualstar Publications,
a divison of Dualstar Entertainment Group, Inc.

Cover photograph courtesy of Dualstar Entertainment Group, Inc. © 2001

The HarperCollins website address is
www.**fire**and**water**.com

1 3 5 7 9 8 6 4 2

ISBN 0 00 714462 8

The authors assert the moral right to be
identified as the authors of the work

Printed and bound in Great Britain by Clays Ltd, St Ives plc

CHAPTER ONE

"I want it," Mary-Kate Burke declared. "I want that snowboard more than I've ever wanted anything in my life."

"And you need it, too," Mary-Kate's friend Campbell Smith agreed. "You have to have your own snowboard if you want to be on the winter sports team."

"I know," Mary-Kate said. "And that's the one I want – right there."

Campbell followed her friend's gaze. The two of them were standing in a crowded sporting goods store at the mall.

Mary-Kate's eyes were glued to a black snowboard. It had bright green-and-blue swirls on

1

it. The name of the board – POWDER POUNDER – was printed in hot pink.

"It's a beauty," Campbell said, admiring it.

"Totally," Mary-Kate said. "And since I made the team, I think it's really unfair that my dad won't buy it for me!"

"Well, making the team wasn't all that hard," Campbell reminded her with a laugh. "All we had to do was sign up."

"True," Mary-Kate admitted.

But that's not the point, she thought. Now that she was on the team, she needed a snowboard. And she needed it before practise started in a few weeks.

Mary-Kate and her twin sister, Ashley, were both students at White Oak Academy for Girls in New Hampshire. Prime snowboarding country was only twenty minutes away by bus.

This year White Oak was starting a winter sports team. No one had to try out for it – even beginners were allowed to join! The coach was going to teach everyone how to snowboard or ski if they didn't already know how.

"Besides," Mary-Kate went on, "I don't want to let the team down."

Campbell grinned. "So now you need a snowboard for the honour of the school," she teased her. "Nice try. And you've been snowboarding only twice in your life!"

"Hey – whose side are you on?" Mary-Kate asked.

"Yours," Campbell said. "So I guess you're going to have to earn the money to buy it. At least it's on sale."

"It is?" Mary-Kate spotted the sign Campbell was looking at. "Wow! It's fifty percent off!"

"Fifty percent off," Campbell muttered. "That makes it one hundred and twenty-five dollars."

Whoa. Mary-Kate didn't have close to that much. She only had fifteen dollars left from her allowance this month.

So what? she thought with a gulp. *I can earn the money. Somehow.*

"Wait here," Mary-Kate said.

She headed towards the young store clerk behind the cash register. He was an older teenage guy with dark curly hair and blue eyes. His name tag said Brad.

Mary-Kate had a quick talk with him and then joined Campbell. She walked out of the store smiling.

"It's all arranged," Mary-Kate explained. "The guy said it was against store policy to hold stuff that isn't paid for. So he's going to put the snowboard in the back room while the manager is away on holiday. But next Saturday it goes back on the floor."

"That's all? Just a week?" Campbell sounded surprised. "You mean you've got to earn all that money in the next six days?"

Mary-Kate nodded. A week. To raise one hundred and ten dollars.

How was she going to do that?

There was only one answer. She'd have to think up a moneymaking scheme of some sort. And fast!

"Let's go," Mary-Kate said. "I've got to talk to Ashley."

Mary-Kate and Campbell took the shuttle bus back to school. When they reached the dorm, a girl in the lounge told them that Ashley was in the Food Management Centre.

"She's baking a batch of her famous jumble-crumble bars," the girl said.

Yum, Mary-Kate thought. Ashley's bars were like blonde brownies jam-packed with chocolate chips. But she also added her own special home-made caramel corn, so they were really chewy.

"Great!" Campbell said, her eyes lighting up. "I'm starving."

The two of them hurried across the tree-lined campus. The last of the autumn leaves had been

4

raked away. The trees were bare and the sky was light grey. A feeling of snow was in the air.

Mary-Kate followed the smell of warm chocolate into the kitchen of the Food Management Centre. She found Ashley and her friends gathered around the counter.

"Ashley, I really need your help," Mary-Kate announced, bursting into the kitchen. "I found the perfect snowboard!"

Ashley and her friends all whirled round to face Mary-Kate.

"Mary-Kate!" Wendy Linden called. "Good thing you're here. Maybe you can talk some sense into your sister. She's torturing us!"

"Torturing you?" Mary-Kate asked. "How?"

"She baked her famous jumble-crumble bars, and she won't even let us have one bite!" Wendy explained.

"Oh, man," Campbell moaned. "Why not?"

"Yeah – why not, Ashley?" Mary-Kate asked.

Ashley pulled the pan of sweet-smelling treats out of the oven. She put them on the counter to cool.

"Because these are for the Head," she said. That's what everyone called Mrs. Pritchard, the headmistress of the school.

"She's having a surprise birthday party for Joan, her secretary," Ashley went on. "She asked me to

5

bake for her."

"Okay, okay, so you have a good reason," Wendy admitted. "You're still torturing us! They smell so . . . "

"Wonderful," Samantha Kramer said, leaning closer to get a good sniff.

Ashley brushed flour off her hands, wiping them on her apron. Even when she was just cooking, she tried to be well dressed. She had on a pair of blue stretch pants and a blue boatneck sweater to match. Her long blonde hair was tied up in twisty knots on top of her head.

"Oh, come on," Campbell moaned. "Mrs. Pritchard won't miss just one."

She reached for the pan of jumble-crumble bars, but Ashley yanked them away.

"She's guarding those things like they're backstage passes to a 4-You concert," Wendy said.

"Ignore her, she's just starving," Ashley told Mary-Kate. "So what's this about a snowboard?"

"I need your help paying for it," Mary-Kate said.

"Why?" Ashley asked.

"It's actually on sale," Mary-Kate explained. "But I still have to earn a hundred and ten dollars by next Saturday."

"Yikes!" Ashley said. "How are you going to do that?"

"I don't know," Mary-Kate said. "That's what I wanted to talk to you about. I thought you could help me come up with some ideas."

"Okay." Ashley shrugged. "I'll try. But first I've got to go meet Heather Langstrom in the newspaper office."

"Heather Langstrom? Who's she?" Mary-Kate asked.

"Heather's a totally popular fourth-former," Wendy answered quickly. "She's the fashion editor of the upper newspaper."

Fourth-former was what they called high school sophomores at White Oak. Mary-Kate and Ashley were in first form. That was the same as seventh grade.

"I can't keep this straight. I thought you were the fashion editor, Ashley!" Campbell complained. "You and Phoebe write the fashion column, don't you?"

Phoebe Cahill was Ashley's roommate.

"Yes," Ashley explained. "But we're on the lower-school newspaper – the *White Oak Acorn.* Heather writes for the upper-school newspaper – the *White Oak Leaf.*"

"So why are you meeting with her?" Mary-Kate asked.

"Because I just found out the most amazing thing!" Ashley said. "Her mom is the editor of *Cool It* magazine!"

"Really? That's awesome!" Samantha Kramer cried.

"What's *Cool It*?" Campbell asked.

Everyone rolled their eyes at her.

Even I know Cool It, Mary-Kate thought. And I'm not a serious fashion addict like Ashley.

"It's only the best teen fashion magazine on the planet," Samantha explained to Campbell. "It came out last year."

"Yeah," Phoebe said. "Even I read it – and they don't feature a single thing I would buy!"

Everyone looked at Phoebe and laughed.

Phoebe was wearing a pair of bright green-and-blue-checked bell-bottom trousers, a scruffy pair of reindeer boots, and an old brown corduroy top. She always dressed in outrageous vintage clothes, stuff she bought at thrift shops. She was totally original – and way cool.

"Anyway," Ashley went on, "Heather's mom edits *Cool It* magazine, so I'm interviewing Heather about it. I'll bet she's met all kinds of models and everything."

"Cool," Mary-Kate said.

"It," Campbell added, making a lame joke.

"Okay, so after you talk to Heather, will you help me think of a way to earn a hundred and ten dollars?" Mary-Kate asked.

"I'll tell you one way to make money," Samantha interrupted. "Get Ashley to bake jumble-crumble bars and you can sell them. I'd pay anything for one of those right now!"

"Me, too," Wendy said, drooling at the bars. "I'll bet lots of people would. You could even sell them to the guys at Harrington."

Harrington was the boys' boarding school down the road from White Oak Academy. The girls had some of their classes at Harrington, and the guys came over to White Oak's campus to hang out in the student U.

"That's brilliant!" Mary-Kate cried. "Will you do it, Ashley?"

"I don't know . . ." Ashley's voice trailed off. "It sounds like a lot of work. I mean, how many would I have to bake?"

"I'm not sure," Mary-Kate admitted. "I'll figure it out later. Please say yes, Ashley? Please? It's the only way I can be on the team. And just think – when everyone hears about this, they'll all start coming to you, to place their orders and stuff. You'll

9

be seriously popular."

Mary-Kate saw her sister's eyes shine, and she knew Ashley liked the idea.

"Okay." Ashley gave in with a shrug. "I'm happy to help you out. I'll bake a few batches."

"You will? That will be fantastic!" Mary-Kate cried. She ran over and gave her sister a hug. "And you won't have to do all the baking yourself. I'll help!"

"Oh, no!" Ashley shook her head fast. "No thanks. You're a disaster in the kitchen. But you can do cleanup. I'll be the chef. You're the dishwasher."

Dishwasher? Okay, Mary-Kate thought. *I'll do whatever it takes to get that snowboard by next week!*

"What are we waiting for?" she said to her sister. "Let's get to work!"

CHAPTER TWO

"Not so fast," Ashley said. She took off her apron and grabbed her coat and scarf. "First I've got to deliver these jumble-crumbles to Mrs. Pritchard. And then I'm meeting Heather. Remember?"

"When you talk to her, find out how we can become models for *Cool It* magazine!" Samantha called.

"That's easy," Phoebe said. "All you have to do is grow six inches."

"With my luck, if I grew six inches, it would be in all the wrong places!" Wendy joked.

"Hurry back," Mary-Kate called to Ashley. "I want to get started baking!"

"Hold on, Mary-Kate," Ashley said. "How are we going to bake without ingredients?"

She raced back into the kitchen and shoved the recipe at her sister. "Take the shuttle bus into town and buy the stuff. I'll be back."

Then she dashed out of the door.

As soon as Ashley had dropped the jumble-crumble bars off in Mrs. Pritchard's office, she turned and crunched through the snow towards the Multi-Purpose Building. It was a small ivy-covered stone building near the arts centre. The *White Oak Acorn's* office was on the first floor. So were the offices for the other newspaper and several other activities.

Ashley peeked into the *Leaf's* office. Heather was sitting on a long table, dangling her legs and reading something out loud. Even sitting down, she looked tall and slender. She had large brown eyes and long, silky blonde hair that fell in her face when she glanced down.

Two other older girls sat listening nearby.

"'Jessica's brown fake-fur skirt made her look like the bear from a Saturday-morning kiddie show,'" Heather read. "'Jake didn't know whether to dance with her or wrestle her to the ground.'"

"That's hilarious!" one of the girls said. "It's like fashion meets sitcom."

12

"Exactly," Heather said. "I'm trying to come up with a new column – fashion and gossip with a humorous twist."

Ashley stepped into the room and waited for them to notice her. When they didn't, she cleared her throat loudly. All three girls looked up.

"Uh, hi," Ashley said.

The girls stared at her for a second without speaking.

"Yes?" Heather finally said.

"Um, I'm Ashley Burke," Ashley said, introducing herself. "I write for the *White Oak Acorn*. I'm supposed to interview you, remember?"

"Oh, right," Heather said.

One of Heather's friends gave Ashley a cold, snooty stare. It was a girl named Emily something. Ashley had seen her in the dining hall. She was always making first-formers feel like little bugs – as if they were annoying pests.

"So what did you want to ask me about?" Heather said.

"Well, I thought I'd write about your mom's magazine," Ashley explained. "But from the insider's point of view."

"Oh." Heather nodded and shrugged. "Okay. Ask away."

Ashley took off her coat and pulled out a pen and notebook. Then she grabbed a chair and glanced over her list of questions.

What I really want to know is: How can I get my face onto the cover of Cool It? Ashley thought.

But she knew better than to ask *that*. Heather would probably just tell her to use glue!

"For starters, how does your mom know what's going to be in style?" Ashley asked.

"That's so lame," Emily said. "Duh. Her mom's the editor in chief! She makes up the styles!"

"Actually, that's not quite true," Heather said. "My mom goes to all the designer runway shows. She sees what's coming out, what's new. Then she decides which clothes to put in the magazine."

"Cool." Ashley nodded.

"And she has a lot of young people working for her," Heather continued. "They go to the fashion shows, too, and then my mom asks their opinions. But that's going to change soon."

"Oh, really?" Ashley said. "How?"

"Well, my mom decided that *Cool It* needs a teen panel," Heather explained.

"What's that?" Ashley was instantly interested.

"It will be a group of five or six teens who give advice and opinions about what's hot, what's in

14

fashion in their part of the country," Heather explained. "She's going to choose a panel from a different school every month."

"And she's starting with White Oak!" one of Heather's friends announced.

"That's awesome!" Ashley said. "I'll bet you'll get to be on the panel for sure."

Heather shook her silky blonde hair. "I can't," she said. "My mom thinks it wouldn't be right to put her own daughter on the panel. But I write stuff for the magazine sometimes and I'm helping her get the panel together. Emily and Briana are trying out for it." Heather nodded towards her two friends.

Wow, Ashley thought. This was the chance she'd been waiting for. It was what she and her friends dreamed about – a chance be part of the *real* fashion world.

"I'd love to try out, too," Ashley said. "What do I have to do?"

Emily laughed. "You can't," she said. "You're too young."

Ashley's face fell. "Well, then how old do you have to be?"

Heather shrugged. "There's no age limit, I guess, but my mom wants upper-school girls. I probably wasn't even supposed to tell you about it."

Ashley straightened her back. Why shouldn't she be able to try out just like everyone else? After all, she and her friends all read *Cool It*.

And they loved it.

And they were teens, for sure.

"I want to try out anyway," Ashley said firmly. "If I don't get on the panel – that's okay. But at least I want to try."

Emily rolled her eyes. "You have to be able to write really well," she said. "Take my word for it – this isn't for first-formers. You've got to write a sample column about fashion and turn it in by Monday."

By Monday! Ashley thought. Today was Saturday. That was only two days away!

"When will the winners be chosen?" Ashley asked.

"On Friday," Heather said. "My mom is coming to White Oak to reveal the results at morning announcements."

"Are there any other requirements?"

"It helps if your English teacher recommends you," Heather said.

No problem, Ashley thought. Mrs. Bloomberg, her English teacher, liked her a lot. She should probably stay on Heather's good side, too. Maybe she would get to help her mom pick out the teen panel.

Ashley closed her notebook and gathered up her stuff.

"Do you mind if we finish this interview later?" she asked Heather. "I really want to get started on my sample column."

"What part of 'you're too young' didn't you understand?" Emily laughed.

But Heather shot Emily a "back off" stare. "Let her try out if she wants," Heather said. "It's not like she's going to hurt anyone else's chances."

Thanks a lot! Ashley thought.

But she didn't really care what Heather said about her now. The only thing that mattered was what Heather thought after she read her sample column!

Which meant it had to be good. Really good.

Ashley was going to have to do the best writing of her life – and on a really short deadline, too.

I just wish I didn't have to bake jumble-crumble bars for Mary-Kate, Ashley thought. *I have to get started right now. I have to write a winning column. Cool It – here I come!*

CHAPTER THREE

"Oh, wow. Butter costs two forty-nine a pound!" Mary-Kate cried. "How am I ever going to pay for all this?"

"Chill. I'll lend you the money," Campbell said. "You can pay me back out of the profits."

Mary-Kate shot her roommate a grateful smile. The two of them pushed a small grocery trolley through the tiny shop in town.

"Thanks," Mary-Kate said. "You're saving my life. But I'm totally freaking out about this! I've got almost forty dollars worth of stuff in here."

She put the butter back in the case and reached for the margarine instead.

"Margarine is cheaper," she told Campbell.

"Okay," Campbell said. "It probably won't make any difference. What else do we need?"

Mary-Kate glanced at the recipe. "Well, it looks like Ashley uses two cups of caramel corn in each batch of jumble-crumbles."

"Whoa," Campbell said. "You're making how many batches?"

"Maybe six or seven," Mary-Kate said. "I haven't figured it out yet."

"Well, how many bars are there in a batch?" Campbell asked.

"Twenty," Mary-Kate answered.

"Okay, so six batches times twenty—" Campbell stopped to do the maths in her head. "That's one hundred and twenty bars. At a dollar each, that would be one hundred and twenty dollars."

"Perfect!" Mary-Kate said.

"Not exactly," Campbell said. "Because you've got to pay for all these ingredients. And when you're done, you'll have spent the fifteen dollars you started with. Plus you'll have to pay me back. And you need one hundred and twenty-five dollars for the board, so—"

"Stop!" Mary-Kate said. "I can't handle all this maths! Let's just get the popcorn and keep moving."

She grabbed eight bags of popcorn from the shelf and dropped them into the shopping trolley. That looked like more than enough.

Then she and Campbell paid for all the groceries and hauled the bags on to the shuttle bus.

"We're back!" Mary-Kate called to Ashley half an hour later. The two girls dragged the heavy bags into the Food Management Centre and heaved them onto the counter. Mary-Kate dusted a few snowflakes off the bags.

"Good," Ashley said. "I cleaned up the kitchen while you were gone. I've got to get this baking finished tonight – because guess what? I'm going to be on a teen panel for *Cool It* magazine!"

"You are?" Mary-Kate's mouth dropped open.

Ashley quickly explained what had happened with Heather. "So I've got to write a sample column right away," Ashley said.

"But first you've got to bake!" Mary-Kate said. "You promised! And I've got fifty dollars worth of brown sugar, margarine, chocolate chips, and popcorn right here!"

"Margarine!" Ashley said. "Why did you get that? I only use butter."

"But it was cheaper," Mary-Kate said.

Ashley shook her head. "They won't taste the same," she said. "And I'm not putting my reputation for perfect jumble-crumble bars on the line just to save a few pennies. What else did you get?"

Before Mary-Kate could answer, Ashley started going through the shopping bags. She pulled out the baking soda. It was on top.

"The recipe calls for baking powder, not baking soda!" Ashley said.

"Are they different?" Mary-Kate asked.

Ashley rolled her eyes and kept looking through the bags. "And you've got way too much popcorn! What were you thinking?"

"The recipe said two cups for each batch," Mary-Kate defended herself.

"That's two cups of popped corn – not two cups of kernels!" Ashley said. "You have to go back to the shop."

Mary-Kate's shoulders slumped. "Okay. But can you get started while I'm gone?" she asked.

"Not without the butter," Ashley reminded her.

Oh, no, Mary-Kate thought. It would be almost dinnertime by the time she got back from her second trip into town.

And after that it would be too late. Ashley

21

wanted to spend the night writing her *Cool It* column.

What am I going to do? Mary-Kate thought. *The weekend is almost half gone – and I haven't even earned a penny yet.*

Ashley curled up on her bed with a brand-new notebook in her lap. The notebook was one of her favourites – the kind with black pages. She pulled out a lavender gel pen, which was the only kind of pen that would show up on the black sheets.

Now what am I going to write about? she thought, staring into her wardrobe for inspiration.

It had to be something about fashion.

Something cool.

And, most important, something that didn't sound too *babyish*.

I know! Ashley thought. STUFF IT: HOW TO PACK (AND WHAT TO TAKE) FOR YOUR BACKPACKING TRIP THROUGH EUROPE.

That wouldn't be too babyish for sure!

The only problem was that other than the title, she didn't have any good ideas.

Yet.

She hopped off her bed and grabbed a pile of fashion magazines from the floor of her wardrobe.

Maybe these will give me some inspiration, she thought, spreading them around her on the bed.

For the next forty minutes, she flipped through the pages and stared.

Nothing came to her.

"What's up?" Phoebe asked, popping in and tossing her raccoon jacket on her bed. "I thought you were supposed to be baking jumble-crumbles for Mary-Kate."

"It's a long story," Ashley said. "I'm baking tomorrow. But guess what? There's a contest to win a spot on a teen panel for *Cool It*, and I'm going to enter!"

"Really?" Phoebe looked interested. "What's the deal?"

"You have to write a fashion column to try out," Ashley explained. "The people who write the five best columns will get picked to be on the panel."

"Wow," Phoebe said. "Maybe I'll enter, too."

Phoebe? Ashley thought. *Okay – I guess that's fair. Even though it means more competition!*

"I'll warn you, though," Ashley said. "They're mostly looking for upper-school girls. Heather's friend trashed the idea of me being on the panel. She said I was 'too young.'"

Phoebe shook her head. "That's not fair."

23

"Tell me about it," Ashley said.

"Well, we'll show them," Phoebe said. "I think I'll write a column about vintage. What do you think?"

"I think that would be perfect!" Ashley said honestly. "You're the vintage queen of White Oak."

But what am I going to write about? she wondered. She knew she had to come up with something good.

Something that would impress Heather – and her mom.

Something so not-young-sounding that they'd pick her even though she was in first form.

And she had less than forty-eight hours to do it!

CHAPTER FOUR

"Ashley? Wake up!" a voice said. "Wake up! It's almost ten o'clock!"

Ashley rolled over in bed and tried to slip back into her dream. It had been a good dream. No, a great one! She was in New York City, giving fashion advice to everyone on the staff of *Cool It*. And then the editor came in and told her she was going to be on the cover of the magazine! She was a model!

But then the dream changed. All of a sudden she was baking jumble-crumble bars in the magazine offices. And they wouldn't let her go home until she baked dozens and dozens and dozens . . .

"Wake up!" Mary-Kate shook Ashley's shoulder. "It's Sunday. We've got to get busy baking!"

25

Go away! Ashley thought, squeezing her eyes shut. She didn't want to bake jumble-crumble bars right now.

She wanted to work on her column for *Cool It*.

Plus she still had to write an article for the *White Oak Acorn*. And she hadn't finished interviewing Heather yet. And she had homework to do!

But Ashley had promised, and she always kept her word.

"Okay," she finally said, sitting up and yawning. She turned her head to see if Phoebe, her roommate, was still asleep. She was sitting up, writing in bed.

Oh, boy, Ashley thought. *She's probably working on her sample for* Cool It. *And I haven't even started mine yet!*

"Look what I've got!" Mary-Kate cried, waving a fistful of papers. "Orders! Campbell put up signs everywhere to advertise the jumble-crumbles and the orders are just streaming in! Everyone wants them – especially the girls in Porter House."

"That makes sense." Ashley nodded. "Everyone in our dorm is desperate for snacks – ever since the microwave in the lounge blew out last week."

"Why won't the school just buy a new one?" Phoebe wondered. "I miss having hot chocolate at night. Especially on cold days like today!"

"Well, I asked Miss Viola about that," Ashley explained. "Not all the dorms have a micro. I guess some girls chipped in and bought that one a few years ago. Miss Viola said if we want a new one, we'll have to buy it ourselves."

Miss Viola was the housemother in Porter House.

"We don't want a new one!" Mary-Kate cried. "We want everyone to be desperate to buy your jumble-crumble bars instead! So hurry up and get dressed. We've got to get to work!"

Ashley showered and hurried to the Food Management Centre and got right to work baking. She made two batches of jumble-crumbles before noon. Then she took off her apron.

"What are you doing?" Mary-Kate cried. "We can't stop now! You haven't filled my orders yet."

"I've got to take a break for lunch," Ashley said. "And I still have to interview Heather."

Mary-Kate moaned. "Okay, about the interview," she said. "But can't you skip lunch? We have so much baking to do!"

Ashley rolled her eyes as she threw on her coat. "I need the energy," she said. "If I don't eat, I'll never get everything done!"

Ashley dashed across campus to the Multi-Purpose Building. Students were building snowmen and having snowball fights all around her. But Ashley couldn't even think about that fun stuff right now. She was way too busy!

Heather was in the *Leaf* office surrounded by five other staff members. Papers and photos were spread out all over the place. The staff were working like mad to meet their deadline.

"Hi!" Ashley said, rushing into the office and rubbing her hands together to warm them from the cold air.

Heather glanced up in a panic. "What?" she said.

Uh-oh, Ashley thought. Bad timing. Heather looked way too busy to talk about her mom's magazine just then.

"Uh, I was just wondering if we could finish that interview . . . sometime," Ashley said.

Heather pushed her silky blonde hair out of her face. "Sure, but not now. I'm going nuts here. I've got a deadline, and I'm supposed to be tutoring my sister."

Heather nodded towards a girl who was sitting on a stool a few feet away. Ashley recognised her from the dining hall. She was another first-former, and her name was Peaches.

Ashley didn't know Peaches very well. She lived in another dorm and was sort of quiet. She didn't hang out with anyone Ashley knew.

"You're tutoring her?" Ashley asked.

"Yeah, sort of. You know – helping her with an article she's writing for *Cool It*," Heather answered quickly without looking up from the papers spread in front of her. "My mom wants Peaches to be more involved with the magazine like I am. And I'm supposed to make that happen – somehow."

Ashley glanced at Peaches, who was frowning. She didn't look as if she wanted to be there at all.

"Writing isn't her thing," Heather said in a low voice. "But my mom thought it would be fun for all of us to work together."

I bet Peaches really does need help, Ashley thought. *She looks like she'd do anything to get out of it.*

"Maybe I could help," Ashley blurted out.

Heather glanced up. "What?"

"Well, I'm really good at writing," Ashley said, trying to make her point. "That's why I'm trying out for a spot on the teen panel for *Cool It*. If you want, maybe I could help Peaches with her article."

Heather gave Ashley a big smile. "That would be fantastic! I am so busy right now. Maybe you two can work it out," she said, turning back to her papers. "And thanks!"

"Sure," Ashley said.

She glanced at Peaches, who was staring at her, waiting. "Well?" Peaches said. "Do you want to go somewhere and work on it now?"

"Now?" Ashley said. "Um . . . I can't really do it right now."

Peaches raised her eyebrows. "When?"

Good question, Ashley thought. How was she ever going to tutor Peaches and write an article for *Cool It* by tomorrow? And write a column for the *White Oak Acorn*? And bake jumble-crumble bars for Mary-Kate? What a mess!

"Can we meet tomorrow after school?" Ashley suggested. "I'll be totally ready to help you then."

"Whatever," Peaches said. "I'll meet you in Heather's dorm room."

"Okay," Ashley said as she headed for the door.

"Oh, Ashley? Wait!" Heather called.

Ashley stopped. "Yes?"

"I hear you're baking jumble-crumble bars," Heather called. "If you have any left over that you want to get rid of, keep us in mind!"

Right, Ashley thought glumly. *Sure thing.*

Free jumble-crumble bars for Heather.

I'll put that right at the top of my list!

CHAPTER
FIVE

"Maybe you should use a bigger pan," Mary-Kate suggested. "Can't you bake two batches at once? This is taking so long!" She glanced nervously at the clock. "At this rate, we're going to miss dinner and be here baking all night."

"We don't have a bigger pan," Ashley said. She wiped her buttery hands on her apron and sighed. Then she put her fourth batch of jumble-crumbles into the oven. "And I am not going to skip dinner, no matter what you say."

This plan isn't working, Mary-Kate thought. No matter how fast Ashley baked, they never seemed to get ahead. The orders came in faster than Ashley could bake the bars. And the ingredients went out faster than Mary-Kate could pay for them!

She had just counted up the money she had earned so far – sixty-seven dollars. But she owed Campbell thirty-five dollars for the ingredients. That meant she had only a thirty-two-dollar profit. And Ashley had already used up more than half the butter and chocolate chips. She'd have to buy more soon.

"Maybe we can cut the bars smaller," Mary-Kate said.

"Good idea," Ashley said. "We could probably get twenty-four out of a batch instead of just twenty."

"Look what I've got!" Campbell shouted, running into the kitchen from outside. "Five more orders for six-packs!"

"Great," Mary-Kate said half-heartedly. But she wasn't really sure she was glad. "From who?"

"From Harrington boys," Campbell said. "They're all hanging out over in the student U. Brian, Elliot, Dylan, Marty Silver, and Josh Martin each ordered a six-pack of jumble-crumble bars for themselves. And a bunch of guys said they'd order more tomorrow, when you come to science class. Plus your cousin, Jeremy, wants four. But he thinks you should give him a discount."

"No discounts!" Mary-Kate declared.

"Right!" Ashley chimed in.

Mary-Kate smiled at her sister. "See? I knew you'd be on my side! You really want me to get that snowboard, don't you?"

"Sure," Ashley answered. "And besides that, I don't want to be baking any longer than I have to. If you start giving discounts, you'll have to sell more bars to make up the difference – and I'll have to bake them!"

"Listen," Mary-Kate said. "You've got to be here to start baking as soon as classes get out tomorrow."

"I can't," Ashley replied. "I'm tutoring Peaches tomorrow afternoon."

Mary-Kate shook her head. "No way," she said. "You don't have time to tutor her. Not if we're going to bake ten batches."

"Ten batches! When did it turn out to be so many?" Ashley asked, horrified.

"When Campbell and I did some more maths," Mary-Kate admitted.

"Oh, no," Ashley said. "I offered to make a few batches of jumble-crumble bars. But I never promised to devote my whole life to buying you a snowboard!"

"Well, this would be going faster if you didn't have to run the whole show yourself!" Mary-Kate shot back. "I offered to help bake, but you wouldn't let me!"

"Well, guess what? I've changed my mind!" Ashley said. She took off her apron and threw it on the counter.

"But what about the orders?" Mary-Kate cried. "People have paid us money!"

"You want jumble-crumble bars?" Ashley called on her way out the door. "Bake them yourself!"

"Oh, boy," Campbell said, rolling her eyes. "You're in big trouble now."

Mary-Kate felt her throat tighten up. How could Ashley just walk out on her that way?

But she also felt guilty. She knew she'd been a little selfish – expecting Ashley to do so much work.

Okay, maybe it was a lot selfish.

"What am I going to do?" Mary-Kate moaned, staring at the kitchen. "This place is a mess!"

Campbell nodded. "And you've got to bake at least three more batches today if you're going to fill all the orders."

"Oh, no," Mary-Kate groaned. She stared at the kitchen in a panic. Then she pulled herself together.

This can't be so hard. Can it? she thought.

At least Ashley left the recipe for her.

"Okay, let's get to work," she declared. She put on the apron and picked up the recipe. "Looks like I've got to make a batch of Ashley's famous caramel corn first. That's the first ingredient. Want to help?"

"I can't," Campbell said. She sounded really sorry. "I've got volleyball practise in ten minutes. But I'll help out when practise is over."

Mary-Kate nodded. "Okay. See you in an hour?"

"Right." Campbell promised on her way out.

When Campbell was gone, Mary-Kate looked around again and sighed. She felt so out of place in a normal-size kitchen – and this one was huge! There were three refrigerators and four stoves.

And the mess from Ashley's baking was spread out on every surface.

Oh, well, she told herself. *All I have to do is follow the instructions. How hard can it be?*

First she popped some popcorn and put it in the only clean bowl she could find. Then she measured out brown sugar and butter for the caramel coating. There were no more clean bowls, so she put the ingredients in the one Ashley had used to make caramel stuff before.

So it's sort of sticky-gooey inside, Mary-Kate thought. *So what? At least the sticky part is just old caramel.*

She put the bowl in the microwave and punched some buttons. While the caramel was cooking, she mixed up the batter for another batch of bars. It took longer than it usually took Ashley. But pretty soon the batter was ready.

"Whoops! I almost forgot to add the caramel corn," Mary-Kate muttered, talking to herself.

She opened the microwave. The brown sugar and butter had turned to a solid sticky mass. It was stuck hard to the inside of the bowl.

"Ewww!" Mary-Kate said. "Now what?"

There was only one thing to do. She warmed up the bowl of caramel stuff again, to melt it. Then she poured it on the popcorn and took a bite. It seemed hard and sticky – not like the caramel Ashley made.

But Mary-Kate didn't care. She had enough caramel corn for three batches of jumble-crumble bars.

She tossed two cups of the corn into the batter and poured the batter into a pan.

"What's burning?" Campbell hurried back into the kitchen from volleyball practise.

"Burning?" Mary-Kate's eyes popped open wide. "Oh, my gosh! The bars! The ones Ashley put in the oven an hour ago!"

Mary-Kate and Campbell ran to the oven and opened it. Smoke and a bad burning smell poured out into the room.

"They're ruined!" Mary-Kate cried.

She grabbed an oven glove and pulled the pan out of the oven.

"What am I going to do?" she moaned.

Campbell tossed her jacket on a chair. "Don't give up, that's for sure," Campbell said. "You want that snowboard, don't you?"

"Definitely," Mary-Kate said.

"Then just keep a picture of the Powder Pounder in your mind," Campbell said. "And let's get to work!"

Campbell rolled up her sleeves to help. For the next three hours, the two of them talked about the snowboarding team while they tried to bake Ashley's jumble-crumble bars.

"I have to learn that spinning jump the coach said he would teach us!" Mary-Kate said. She stirred in some sugar.

"Since this is the team's first year I don't think there'll be that many people on the team," Campbell said. "We'll probably get lots of attention."

"But first we have to bake some yummy jumble-

37

crumble bars!" Mary-Kate put in.

Mary-Kate's first batch was anything *but* yummy. She was so worried about burning the bars again, she didn't bake them long enough. They were so mushy that when she tried to cut them, they just fell apart.

The second batch looked okay – until she tasted some crumbs from the pan.

"Blechh," Mary-Kate said. "There's something wrong with this stuff."

Campbell took a bite. "They're not sweet," she said. "They taste like you forgot the sugar."

Mary-Kate slapped her forehead. "Sugar? Oh, my gosh, you're right! I think I left it out," Mary-Kate admitted.

With a huge sigh, she dumped the whole batch of bars into the bin.

But her third batch of bars looked good. And the crumbs in the pan tasted fine.

"I think these are winners!" she announced to Campbell.

"Thank goodness, because I'm exhausted!" Campbell said. "Let's go get some dinner."

Mary-Kate checked the clock. It was seven twenty. The dining hall would close in ten minutes.

"You go," Mary-Kate said. "I want to deliver

these to my customers."

Mary-Kate hurried over to the student U with her list of orders. Her arms ached from mixing batter for three hours. And her stomach was growling with hunger. But at least she felt proud.

I did it! she thought. *I baked Ashley's famous treats! And if I can keep it up, I'll earn the money for the snowboard – somehow.*

A gang of guys crowded around when they saw her step into the game room of the student U.

"I bought six!" Josh Martin called.

"I know," Mary-Kate said, happily handing him six of the individually wrapped bars.

"I ordered six, too!" Elliot called.

"I paid for two!" Elise Van Hook said.

The guys and girls clamoured round her, grabbing. Mary-Kate couldn't help beaming with pride. "I baked these myself!" she announced as she passed out the jumble-crumble bars to her friends.

Then she sank into a soft overstuffed chair and sighed. She was so tired and hungry, she couldn't move. She was definitely too wiped out to walk back to her dorm.

But at least it's done! Mary-Kate thought as she watched Josh Martin unwrap one of her treats and bite into it. *That's all that matters.*

"Ouch!" Josh cried, holding his face.

"What's wrong?" Mary-Kate wondered out loud. She quickly jumped up from the chair.

"I broke a filling on your brownie thing!" Josh yelled, marching over to her. He pulled a piece of metal out of his mouth.

"Sorry," Mary-Kate stammered. "What happened?" She hoped no one else would hear Josh complaining.

"I don't know," Josh said. His voice was getting louder. "The popcorn-caramel stuff is way too hard!"

The caramel corn? Oh, yeah, Mary-Kate thought. *I guess I microwaved it too long.*

"I'm going to have to get a new filling," Josh said. He shoved the other jumble-crumble bars back at her. "Here," he said. "I want my money back."

"Okay, okay." Mary-Kate glanced around. Most people were either playing a video game or watching movies, so they didn't notice. Mary-Kate reached into her pocket and gave Josh six dollars. "Sorry," she repeated.

"Whatever," Josh said, still holding his face.

Mary-Kate ran out of the student U as fast as she could. *I hope he doesn't make me pay for the filling, too!* she thought.

CHAPTER SIX

She raced back to her dorm and found Campbell in their room, eating a sandwich.

"This is all they had left in the dining hall," Campbell said. "Ham sandwiches with pimento cheese. It's pretty gross, but I brought you one anyway. I figured you were starving."

"Thanks," Mary-Kate said, closing the door behind her. "I am."

She flopped on to her bed and unwrapped the sandwich quickly. Campbell passed her a box of apple juice to go with it.

"So how much money have you made so far?" Campbell asked.

41

Mary-Kate shook her head. "Don't even ask. It's more like how much money have I lost?"

"Wow," Campbell said sympathetically. "Is there anything I can do?"

Before Mary-Kate could answer, there was a knock at their door.

Campbell opened it.

Rebecca Duncan was standing there with one hand on her hips – and a half-eaten jumble-crumble bar in the other. "Your jumble things are too chewy," she said, thrusting the bar at Mary-Kate. "I can't eat this. The caramel corn is totally sticking to my teeth!"

"Oh . . . uh, sorry," Mary-Kate said. "Uh, I think the next batch will be better. I'll give you another one tomorrow. Free."

"No thanks," Rebecca said. "I think I want my money back." She turned and glanced over her shoulder into the hall. "And so do they!"

What? Mary-Kate's heart started pounding. She jumped up off her bed. Who?

But as soon as she reached the door, she saw the answer. There were five other people lined up outside her room!

"Sorry, but we can't eat these things," Elise complained, holding her half-eaten bar out to Mary-

Kate. "It's like chewing dried glue!"

"How would you know?" Campbell asked. "Have you ever eaten glue?"

"You want proof?" Elise shot back. She offered the remains of the jumble-crumble bar to Campbell. "Here – try it. I dare you!"

"Okay, okay," Mary-Kate said, holding up her hands. "Never mind. I'll give you your money back." Then she spotted Wendy standing in line. "Why are you here? You didn't buy any bars."

"The guys aren't allowed in our dorm," Wendy explained. "So they sent me over. Elliot and Seth want their money back, too. Sorry, Mary-Kate," she added sheepishly.

Mary-Kate's heart sank. *This can't be happening,* she thought.

But it was. And there was nothing she could do but give back the cash.

She almost wanted to cry as she stood in the hall, passing out dollar bills. When it was over, she had given back twenty-three of the twenty-four dollars she had earned on that batch.

Why not all twenty-four? she wondered. At least someone must have liked my jumble-crumble bars.

She hurried down the hall to Ashley's room. Ashley was sitting at her desk, working on her article for *Cool It*.

"Ashley, you've got to help me," Mary-Kate begged, racing into the room. "I'm sorry I was so bossy, honestly I am. But I was desperate. And I'm even more desperate now. Please, please, please, will you start baking again? Tomorrow afternoon?"

"I just can't," Ashley said. "I've got to tutor Peaches tomorrow. Remember?"

"Oh, right. Well, how about after you tutor her?" Mary-Kate begged.

Ashley shook her head. "Sorry, but I've got homework. Tons. And I'll probably still be working on the fashion column for the *Acorn*. I really wish I could help you out, Mary-Kate – honestly I do. But I'm swamped."

"But, Ashley," Mary-Kate moaned, pleading even harder. "This is my only chance to be on the winter sports team. And I just can't bake those bars. You know I'm a disaster in the kitchen. The Food Management Centre looks like a tornado came through."

Ashley laughed. "The weather bureau should give names to the messes you make – like they do for hurricanes!" She thought for a minute. "Maybe you can come up with another way to earn the money," she suggested. She gave Mary-Kate a sympathetic look. "Look, I really am sorry, but I just don't have time."

Mary-Kate started to leave the room.

Then she noticed something in the wastepaper basket beside Phoebe's desk. It was a jumble-crumble bar – with one bite taken out of it.

"What's that?" Mary-Kate asked, pointing into the bin.

"Oh, Phoebe bought it from Elliot," Ashley explained. "She couldn't eat it – but she didn't want to hurt your feelings."

"So that's where the last one went," Mary-Kate mumbled, feeling worse than ever.

And that's where my dreams of getting a snowboard are going, too, she thought.

Straight into the bin!

CHAPTER SEVEN

"There she is," Ashley whispered to Phoebe.

"Who?" Phoebe asked.

"Peaches," Ashley said. "Shh."

Ashley and Phoebe had just come out of their last class on Monday afternoon. Peaches Langstrom was about ten feet in front of them, making her way through the hall towards the big oak front door.

"I like her style," Phoebe whispered. "She looks almost French."

Ashley checked her out. Peaches was wearing a navy-blue wool stadium jacket – the kind that had a hood and brown wooden buttons on the front. But she wore it so far back on her shoulders, it was almost falling off, like a cape.

46

Her short bobbed blonde hair was silky like her sister Heather's. But the cut was short and blunt, with a blunt fringe.

"Well, of course you think she looks cool," Ashley whispered. "She looks like someone out of the fifties."

"Are you going to catch up with her?" Phoebe asked. "I mean, you're supposed to tutor her right now, aren't you? She's getting away."

"I was hoping to beat her to Heather's room," Ashley admitted. "So I could see if Heather knew anything else about the teen panel. I turned my article in this morning."

"Me, too," Phoebe said.

"I hope we both get picked," Ashley said. "If I get a chance, I'll put in a good word for you with Heather."

"Well, you'd better hurry," Phoebe said. "I'll see you later."

A cold blast of air greeted the girls as Phoebe held the door open for Ashley. Ashley turned left when she got outside, and Phoebe turned right.

Ashley followed Peaches, who was way ahead of her on the walkway. She was making a beeline for her sister Heather's dorm.

Heather lived in Plymouth Hall, the nicest dorm on campus. It was an old mansion with a marble staircase and high ceilings. A lot of upper-school girls lived there.

Two older girls in the lobby directed her to Heather's room. It was upstairs, across from the staircase.

"Knock, knock," Ashley said, rapping on the open door.

Heather was sitting at her desk. Peaches had tossed her coat and books on her sister's bed.

"Oh, hey! Come on in!" Heather said eagerly.

Wow, Ashley thought as she stepped into the older girl's room. *This is so great!*

The high ceilings and two walls of the room were draped with long pieces of gauzy fabric in two tones of red. A third wall was completely covered from top to bottom with fashion photographs and articles. The fourth wall had windows.

"Hey," Peaches said softly, giving Ashley a shy smile.

"Hi." Ashley smiled back. "I love your room," she said to Heather.

"Yeah, thanks." Heather motioned Ashley towards the bed. "Uh, can you guys work over there? I've got to do my history homework."

"Sure," Ashley said with a shrug.

Peaches moved her coat, and Ashley sat down on the edge of the bed beside her. "What's your article about?" she asked Peaches.

"Who knows?" Peaches answered, sounding bored.

"She's supposed to write a funny column about what to wear on a first date," Heather said.

"That sounds good," Ashley said. "Do you have any ideas?"

"No," Peaches said. "Except I'd never wear that. It's so corny." She pointed to a magazine clipping on Heather's wall.

Ashley jumped up and ran over to the wall of photos. It was a picture of Ariel Crenshaw wearing a short slinky black dress. She was a famous model who had been on the cover of *Cool It* magazine.

It was signed: "To Heather, a friend for life – Ariel."

"Oh, my gosh, you know Ariel Crenshaw?" Ashley cried, whirling towards Heather.

Heather nodded. "She hangs out at our apartment in New York all the time," Heather said. "She thinks my mom is her fairy godmother or something."

"What's she like?" Ashley asked.

Heather shrugged. "She's, um, sort of giggly."

"I'd love to interview her," Ashley said. "I mean, I'll bet I could write a great article about how she got started in modelling."

"She started in nappies," Heather said with a laugh. "Not too glamorous. She's been a model ever since she was nine months old."

"No wonder she's so good," Ashley said. "So do you hang out at your mom's office all the time in the summer?"

"Sometimes," Heather said. "I'm going to do an internship this summer in the layout department."

Wow, Ashley thought. *That would be so cool!*

"Speaking of the magazine," Ashley said, "I'm still hoping to get on the teen panel. I turned in my sample article this morning. It's all about the rules for borrowing other people's clothes."

"Do you do that a lot?" Heather asked, glancing at Ashley sideways.

"Uh, no," Ashley said. "But I definitely know what the rules are."

Heather laughed. "Well, good luck," she said. "You and about fifty other people are applying to be on the panel, so don't get your hopes up."

Right, Ashley thought.

Ashley asked Heather all about the magazine and what it was like living in New York.

Finally Peaches stood up and put on her coat. "I've got a choir practice," she said. "I've got to go."

Whoops! I totally forgot about her! Ashley realized.

"I'm sorry," she said quickly. "We didn't work on your article yet!"

"Yeah. Well, you've been ignoring me the whole time," Peaches pointed out.

Ashley's face turned red. "Well, can we do it tomorrow?" she asked.

Peaches made a face. "I guess."

"How about in your room next time," Heather suggested. "I'm not getting anything done with you guys hanging out in here anyway."

"Okay," Peaches said. "Tomorrow after class?"

Ashley nodded. "Tomorrow."

Then she picked up her own things and followed Peaches out of the dorm.

I'd better shape up and really help her, Ashley told herself. *Or Heather and her mom will think I'm not reliable.*

And then they'll never put me on the panel!

CHAPTER EIGHT

"How about fortune-telling?" Campbell joked to Mary-Kate. The two of them were eating dinner in the dining hall on Monday night. "Maybe you could make money that way."

"Madame Mary-Kate, Reader of Palms," Mary-Kate said in a deep, mysterious voice. "I don't think so."

"How about a dog-walking service?" Elise suggested. "Charge money to walk the teachers' dogs after class."

Mary-Kate took a bite of salad and shook her head. "There are only three teachers who live on campus and have dogs," she said, chewing. "And I have only four days left. I'd have to charge—"

"About ten dollars a day from each teacher," Cheryl Miller piped up. Cheryl was the maths whiz in the group.

"Ten dollars a day? No one would pay that much just to have their dogs walked!" Mary-Kate said with a sigh.

She popped a Brussels sprout into her mouth.

"Besides," Cheryl added, "if we could earn a hundred dollars that easily, we should buy a new microwave for the dorm instead. We need that more than you need a snowboard."

"Seriously," Campbell agreed. "I mean, look at us. We're eating Brussels sprouts!"

Samantha nodded and laughed. "I know," she said. "But at least they're food. We can't make microwave popcorn, or heat up old pizza. Every night I go back to my room and starve!"

"Okay, okay. We need a microwave," Mary-Kate agreed. "But first I need to buy a snowboard so I can stay on the winter sports team!"

Just then a fifth-form girl walked past their table. She was wearing a T-shirt that said SKI NEW HAMPSHIRE – 'SNO KIDDING.

"That shirt is pretty cool," Campbell said. "I wonder if they have one that says SNOWBOARD NEW HAMPSHIRE – 'SNO KIDDING. If they do,

I'm going to get one when we go to the slopes."

"I could make you one," Mary-Kate offered. "My dad just sent me a package of iron-on transfer paper, so I can make my own T-shirt designs. It works with my ink-jet printer."

"He did?" Cheryl's eyes lit up. "Well, why don't you do one of those print-your-own-T-shirt businesses? You could make money that way."

"Definitely!" Campbell agreed, getting excited. "I'll bet you could design cool logos and then iron them on to T-shirts!"

"But T-shirts are expensive," Mary-Kate said. "And I'm already in the hole for the chocolate chips!"

"Don't buy new T-shirts," Cheryl said. "Just make the transfers and iron them on to T-shirts that people already have."

"That's brilliant!" Mary-Kate exclaimed. "How much could I charge?"

"Well, I'd pay five dollars for a T-shirt that said PORTER HOUSE PRINCESS," Cheryl answered.

"I'd pay five dollars for one that said NO MORE BRUSSELS SPROUTS!" Samantha joked. "I'd wear it to dinner every night for a week."

"I love it!" Mary-Kate said. "I'll make a T-shirt for myself, too. The shirt will advertise my business!"

"Just don't make one that says I BAKED IT MYSELF," Elise teased.

"Don't remind me," Mary-Kate said. "I never want to see the inside of another oven as long as I live."

As soon as dinner was over, Mary-Kate and Campbell hurried back to their room. Mary-Kate took out a big pad of paper and started coming up with ideas. She wrote down:

SUGAR 'N' SPICE
GOTTA DANCE
PORTER HOUSE PRINCESS!
SOCCER BABE
BORN TO PARTY
MY BOYFRIEND IS A HARRINGTON HUNK

"How about HARRINGTON HOTSHOTS," Campbell suggested. "Those Harrington guys all think they are."

"Good one," Mary-Kate said.

"Maybe you could add a picture of a gorilla to the Harrington logo," Campbell said. "Guys go ape for stuff like that."

"Ha-ha," Mary-Kate said.

Ashley poked her head into Mary-Kate's room. "What's up?" she asked.

"I'm going into the T-shirt business!" Mary-Kate announced. "To earn money for the snowboard."

"Excellent!" Ashley said. "I'll buy one that says COOL IT!" Ashley offered. "But only if I win the contest."

"How are your chances looking?" Campbell asked.

Ashley thought about it. "I can't tell yet," she admitted.

"Maybe you need a T-shirt that says I TUTORED PEACHES LANGSTROM . . . AND ALL I GOT WAS THIS STUPID T-SHIRT," Mary-Kate joked.

"Ha-ha." Ashley frowned. "Not funny. Not funny at all."

CHAPTER NINE

"Peaches, are you here?" Ashley called, stepping into Peaches' dorm room.

This is amazing, Ashley thought as she looked around. This room was as cool as Heather's.

Peaches had taped four bamboo poles to the corners of her bed frame. They stood straight up, like a tall canopy frame. Then she had wrapped the poles with tiny white twinkle lights. The lights were also strung from pole to pole, making a rectangle of light.

There was a fuzzy white fake bearskin rug on the floor. On her notice board she had pictures of horses.

"Oh, hi," Peaches said, clearing off her bed so

they'd have a place to sit.

"I like your room," Ashley said, putting her coat and books on Peaches' chair. "I love the twinkle lights."

"Yeah," Peaches said. "Me, too. Anyway, I wanted to tell you yesterday – you don't have to do this if you don't want to. I mean, I don't care about writing a stupid article for my mom's magazine. So you don't have to waste your time, you know?"

"Oh, I don't mind," Ashley said. "I love to write."

"Really?" Peaches made a face and shook her head. "Not me. My mom always says that ever since I was little, I thought the three R's were reading, riding, and 'rithmetic.'"

"Funny," Ashley said. "So you're really into horses?"

"Big time," Peaches nodded.

"I'm kind of a wimp when it comes to oversize mammals." Ashley shuddered. "I don't like anything that outweighs me by more than two hundred pounds!"

She sat down on Peaches' bed. "So, about your article. You're supposed to write about what not to wear on a first date, right?"

Peaches nodded and handed Ashley her first draft of the article. "I've never even been on a date," Peaches admitted. "How am I supposed to write about going on one?"

"Easy!" Ashley said. "Just use your imagination. I'll bet that's what your mom wanted when she gave you the assignment."

"No," Peaches said. "It was Heather's idea."

Peaches sounds so grumpy every time she mentions Heather's name, Ashley thought.

"Don't you get along with your sister?" Ashley asked.

"Oh, yeah," Peaches said quickly. "I mean, she's fine. But I hate the fact that she and my mom are so much alike. They're both really good at writing, and really into fashion, and I'm not."

"Yeah." Ashley nodded. "I guess that would be hard – trying to keep up with her."

"It is," Peaches said.

"Mary-Kate has the same problem – trying to keep up with me," Ashley joked.

Peaches laughed, but she shook her head. "It's not funny," she said. "My mom and Heather are constantly trying to change me. They want me to be just like them – fashion queens. But deep down, they just think of me as the person who spilled peaches all over my dress when I was five."

"Oh," Ashley said. "Is that how you got your name?"

Peaches nodded. "We were supposed to be in a mother-daughter fashion show," she explained. "Me, my mom, and Heather. The show was being held in a fancy restaurant. We were supposed to eat lunch first and then model our clothes on the runway. I ordered a bowl of canned peaches in syrup and knocked it over. It spilled all down the front of my dress."

"Nightmare," Ashley said.

"Yeah." Peaches nodded. "It was really embarrassing – even for a five-year-old. I was such a mess, I couldn't be in the fashion show. And the worst part was that ever since, everyone's called me Peaches. I hate it. My real name is Julia."

"I'll never call you Peaches again," Ashley said.

"Thanks," Julia said with a warm smile. She was quiet for a minute. "And you know what's even worse?" she went on. "Heather isn't really so perfect. But everyone thinks she is."

She looks perfect to me! Ashley thought. But she wasn't going to say so.

"I mean, I know Heather is the fashion goddess of White Oak," Julia went on. "But she doesn't always do everything right. You should have seen her two years ago. She showed up at our cousin's wedding in a dress with little bells sewn to the bottom of the skirt. The bells kept jingling all through the ceremony. Everyone was ready to kill her!"

Ashley laughed. "Big mistake, right?" she joked.

"Right," Julia said, laughing. "Big mistake. But did everyone start calling her Bell Girl or something after that? No way. Heather can make mistakes and get away with it."

"Well, forget Heather," Ashley announced. "This time you're going to write the best article your mother has ever seen. And I'm going to help you!"

"But I don't really want to write the article," Julia pointed out. She glanced at the clock. "And besides, I'm supposed to go to the library in a few minutes to finish a homework assignment."

"Do you mind if I just sit here and work on your article?" Ashley asked. "Then I can leave it for you when I'm done."

Julia shrugged. "If you want." She began to gather up her things. "Oh, by the way," she said. "Could you give this to your sister?" She held out five dollars to Ashley. "I ordered a T-shirt logo from her."

"Sure," Ashley said as Julia headed for the door. Then Ashley turned to the paper and began to read.

"Wear whatever you want on a first date," Ashley read aloud. "Why do there have to be any rules?"

Wow, Julia really needs my help, Ashley thought. *I'm sure she won't mind if I make a few changes.* She crossed out some of Julia's essay. Then she crossed out some more and began writing.

First-Date Fashion 101

The big thing about first dates is: They're scary enough without freaking out about what to wear. But, hey, don't stress. If you follow a few simple rules, you can stay cool and look hot!

This rule is pretty obvious, but we can't say it often enough: if you're going out for pizza, don't wear white! Actually, this is true for all kinds of Italian food. So, head off a headache by sticking to darker colours!

Also, make sure your outfit fits well. How can you concentrate on his dreamy blue eyes if you're constantly tugging on your tube top? Comfort is key!

But remember, you'll be fine whatever you wear. Just be yourself!

The article will be great, Ashley thought. Now Julia won't feel bad around Heather ever again!

CHAPTER TEN

"Campbell! Guess what? I got five orders!" Mary-Kate called, dashing into the lounge in Porter House.

"Way to go!" Campbell said without glancing up from her video game.

Phoebe was sitting in the corner, reading a book of poetry. Her head snapped up. "Don't tell me you're baking those jumble-crumble bars again!" she said.

"No, no, no," Mary-Kate answered quickly. "I've got a new business. I'm selling T-shirt designs. Want to buy one? It can say anything you want."

"I'll think about it," Phoebe agreed.

"Good," Mary-Kate said. "See you later. I've got to get to work printing these transfers!"

Mary-Kate dashed upstairs carrying five T-shirts from her customers. One was from Brian Parks at Harrington. He wanted the Harrington Hotshots logo. Marty Silver had come up with his own idea. He wanted DUDE WITH 'TUDE.

Plus she had three orders from White Oak girls. Mary-Kate sat down at her computer and started working. She loved choosing different fonts for the words, and adding pictures, too.

It took about two hours to make all five transfer designs. Then she loaded the special transfer paper into her ink-jet printer.

When she had printed the transfers, she went to Miss Viola.

"Miss Viola, may I borrow the iron?" Mary-Kate asked.

"Of course," Miss Viola answered. "But be careful. You're allowed to use it only in the laundry room, remember. And never leave it on when you're not right there."

"Don't worry," Mary-Kate promised.

I may be a klutz in the kitchen, Mary-Kate thought. *But I'm a wizard with a pile of dirty clothes!*

Mary-Kate hurried to the laundry room with her things. She plugged in the iron and let it get hot. Then she started ironing on the first transfer –

the one that said HARRINGTON HOTSHOTS.

"Let's see," Mary-Kate muttered, reading the instructions one more time. "It says the shiny side goes on top."

She pressed hard and ironed for a full minute, counting to sixty just like it said on the package.

Then she lifted the iron and peeled the backing paper away.

"Oh, no!" Mary-Kate cried when she saw what she had done.

The words on the shirt were backwards. Brian's T-shirt now had a bright red logo on it that said: STOHSTOH NOTGNIRRAH.

"Oooh," Mary-Kate moaned. "I was supposed to print it backwards on the printer so it would come out forwards when I iron it on!"

She unplugged the iron and ran back up to her room.

All the transfers are wrong, she realised. She'd have to print them all again.

She went back to the computer program and clicked on Reverse. That made the words and pictures appear backwards on her screen. Then she printed the transfers again.

"That's better," Mary-Kate said. She was trying very hard not to feel bad about her mistake.

She hurried back to the laundry room and started ironing on another transfer.

This time, she was working on Summer Sorenson's shirt. It said TOO HOT TO HANDLE.

"Stop the presses!" Ashley said as she raced into the room. "Or should I say stop the pressing!"

"Ha-ha." Mary-Kate laughed at Ashley's joke. "What's up?"

"Did you already do Julia's shirt?" Ashley asked.

"Whose?" Mary-Kate said.

"Julia Langstrom's – I mean Peaches'. Her real name is Julia," Ashley said.

"No," Mary-Kate said. "Hers is next."

"Well, I have a great idea for it," Ashley said. "She loves horses – so it should say HORSING AROUND. Hey, what do I smell? Is something burning?"

"Yikes!" Mary-Kate cried, lifting the iron quickly. "You talked to me and I forgot to count!"

Mary-Kate gasped when she saw what had happened to Summer's shirt. There was a big brown scorch mark on the front. It was shaped exactly like the iron.

"Whoa," Ashley said, staring at the mistake. "Maybe that one should have said BURNING FOR LOVE or something."

Mary-Kate closed her eyes. *What am I going to do?* she thought. *I keep messing up!*

She opened her eyes. "Ashley," she began in a nice, pleading tone of voice. "Do you want to stick around and help me make sure I . . . ?"

Ashley shook her head and backed out of the room. "Sorry, I can't. I've got to go write my article for the *Acorn!*" she said.

Mary-Kate sighed. *I don't blame her,* she thought. *She already baked her brains out for me.*

And for what? Nothing! I still don't have the money for the snowboard.

Okay, Mary-Kate told herself. *Concentrate. You can do this!*

For the next shirt, she was very careful to make sure the logo was forwards, not backwards. And that it was right side up. And that she didn't scorch the shirt.

But unfortunately, the T-shirt was inside out, and Mary-Kate didn't notice. She ironed it on the inside of the shirt instead of the outside!

"Hi!" a voice in the doorway said.

Mary-Kate glanced up glumly. Her shoulders sagged. "Hi, Phoebe," she replied. "What's up?"

"I've decided to order a T-shirt," Phoebe said. "And I know what I want it to say."

"You do? That's great!" Mary-Kate asked. "What's your logo?"

But Phoebe didn't answer. She was staring at the pile of messed-up shirts on the table beside Mary-Kate. The scorched one was on top. The STOHSTOH NOTGNIRRAH shirt was right beside it.

"Uh, on second thoughts, I'm not sure," Phoebe said. "I'm still thinking about it. Bye!"

Phoebe turned and hurried out of the laundry room as fast as she could.

"Thanks a lot," Mary-Kate muttered.

She stared at the two remaining shirts – the ones she still had to work on. One was Julia Langstrom's. The other was Wendy's.

Even if I don't mess them up, I'm still in deep trouble, Mary-Kate thought.

I'll probably have to pay Brian, Marty, and Summer for the shirts I ruined. And I'll definitely have to give them their money back.

And I'm still in debt from the jumble-crumble bars!

What am I going to do? she wondered.

There were only three days left to raise one hundred and twenty-five dollars.

After that, her hopes of getting a new snowboard would melt away like snow in the spring.

CHAPTER ELEVEN

"Ashley, come on," Phoebe called from the doorway. "We're going to be late!"

"Just one more sec," Ashley mumbled from deep inside her wardrobe. "I'm trying to find a certain scarf. It makes me look older."

Phoebe squinted. "I don't get it. Why do you want to look older?"

"When they announce the *Cool It* contest winners this morning and I have to walk up on to the stage, I don't want to look like a first-form geek," Ashley explained.

"Ohhh," Phoebe said. "You mean so Emily, Heather's friend, won't bother you again?"

Ashley nodded as she ducked out of her

wardrobe. She had a colourful scarf in her hand.

"You're pretty sure you're going to win?" Phoebe asked.

"Definitely!" Ashley said. "I worked so hard on that article!"

Ashley smiled to herself, thinking about her column. STAY OUT OF MY WARDROBE: THE RULES FOR BORROWING AND LENDING CLOTHES by Ashley Burke.

It was filled with good advice that definitely didn't sound too young.

"Well, if we don't hurry, we're going to miss the morning announcements altogether!" Phoebe complained.

"Okay, okay!" Ashley said. "I've got it. Let's go!"

She tossed the scarf around the neck of her black turtleneck sweater and knotted it. Then she followed Phoebe out of the door.

The girls hurried to the auditorium, where the morning announcements were read aloud from the stage. White Oak students and teachers were scattered throughout the seats.

Ashley spotted Mary-Kate sitting with Campbell and Cheryl Miller about halfway down the rows.

"Hi," Ashley said, excited. She nudged her sister, who was sitting on the aisle. "Move over. I want to sit where I can get out easily."

"How come?" Mary-Kate asked.

"In case I have to go up on the stage to say something when they announce the winners," Ashley explained.

Mary-Kate rolled her eyes. "Wake up, Ashley. This isn't Hollywood or anything! They aren't giving you a gold statue, you know."

"But if they do, be sure to thank us when you make your acceptance speech," Campbell teased. "You know – 'I want to thank all the little people who helped me get where I am today.'"

Ashley took the seat on the aisle, and Phoebe sat beside her.

"Good morning, girls," Mrs. Pritchard said into the microphone on the stage. "We are very lucky to have one of our girls' mothers with us this morning. So please, let's hear a nice welcome for Mrs. Andrea Langstrom."

Everyone clapped.

"As many of you know," the Head went on, "Mrs. Langstrom is the editor in chief of *Cool It* magazine. We're all proud and honoured that she's decided to choose her first teen panel for the magazine from our student body. Girls who wanted to be considered for the panel had to write a sample article and get recommendations from their teachers. Mrs. Langstrom – are you ready to announce the winners?"

Heather's mother nodded and walked to the microphone. She was wearing black jeans and a black turtleneck sweater. And she had a colourful scarf around her neck.

Just like me! Ashley thought.

"Creepy," Mary-Kate whispered, leaning towards Ashley. "You and Heather's mom are dressed alike!"

"I know," Ashley said, suddenly feeling weird about it.

"Well, you wanted to look older!" Phoebe teased her.

"Not thirty years older!" Ashley complained.

She held her breath. Mrs. Langstrom was talking all about the magazine and the teen panel. About how the girls chosen would get their pictures in the magazine, and would write about fashion at White Oak.

"And now to announce the five winners," Mrs. Langstrom said.

Ashley sat up straighter and smiled.

"Our teen panel will consist of Annabelle Ratajcek, Nina Sloan, Emily Cloninger . . ."

Ashley flinched. That was Heather's snooty friend!

She glanced at Emily, who was smiling smugly.

". . . Martine Waggoner, and Phoebe Cahill!" Mrs. Langstrom said, finishing the list.

"I made it!" Phoebe cried, lurching forward in her seat.

Was that it? Ashley thought. *Was that really the end of Mrs. Langstrom's list?*

Everyone was clapping, and someone next to Ashley was saying something, but she didn't hear it. And Mary-Kate was reaching over to pat her on the arm, but she didn't feel it.

Her mind was a blur and her throat was closing up. She felt as if she was going to cry.

All she could think was *I didn't make it.*

I didn't get on the teen panel.

I didn't get chosen for the coolest job in the universe – and Phoebe and Emily did!

CHAPTER
TWELVE

"Ashley, are you okay?" Mary-Kate asked, poking her head into her sister's room that night. Mary-Kate was on her way to the slumber party in the lounge that she and Campbell had organised. A bunch of girls were going to sleep on the floor and hang out there all night.

"I guess," Ashley said. She was lying on her bed. "I'm just disappointed, that's all. I really wanted to be on the panel."

"I can't believe they didn't pick you," Mary-Kate said. "Your article was really good."

"Did you think so?" Ashley asked. "Honestly. Tell me the truth."

Mary-Kate nodded again. "Most of it was great –

although some of it didn't sound like you. It sounded like you were trying to prove you were older or something."

"I was," Ashley admitted.

"Oh, well," Mary-Kate said with a shrug. "Next time. Anyway, are you coming to the party?"

"Yeah, I'll be down in a few minutes," Ashley said.

"Good." Mary-Kate smiled. "We'll drown our sorrows in cola and crisps. I'll see you downstairs. Bring lots of pillows!"

Mary-Kate hurried down the steps to the lobby of Porter House. "Pizza time!" she announced, waving a coupon in her hand. "I'm too broke to chip in for it, though, so this is my share – the coupon. We can get two large cheese pizzas for the price of one."

Phoebe took the coupon and went to phone for the pizza.

Mary-Kate flopped down on to her sleeping bag on the floor. "Everyone has to make me feel better tonight," she announced. "Because I have just had the worst week of my life!"

"Tell me about it!" Summer said, pointing to the T-shirt she was wearing. It was the one Mary-Kate had ruined. There was a big scorch mark on the front.

Everyone laughed.

"Actually, TOO HOT TO HANDLE sort of goes with that scorch mark, doesn't it?" Mary-Kate joked.

"Ha-ha," Summer said.

"So what happened?" Elise asked Mary-Kate. "Did you ever get the money for the snowboard?"

Mary-Kate shook her head. "I called the store today and begged the guy to give me one more week," she explained. "But he couldn't. He's putting it back on the floor tomorrow. So I guess I have to quit the team."

Everyone was quiet for a minute.

"I'll miss you at practice every week," Campbell said. "Hey! Maybe Coach won't notice if we share a board."

"Unless we tell him we're Siamese twins, I don't think that will work," Mary-Kate said with a smile. "But thanks."

For the next hour, Mary-Kate and her friends talked about school and their favourite topic: the Harrington guys.

Finally the pizza arrived. But it was cold when it got there. As usual.

"Why can't they keep it hot in the delivery car?" Samantha complained.

"Because it's only two degrees outside!" Phoebe explained.

"If we had a microwave in here, we could heat it up," Campbell said. She sighed.

"If we had a microwave, we could do lots of things," Phoebe agreed.

"I am so starving for popcorn," Wendy moaned.

"Me, too," Samantha agreed.

"Me, three," Ashley said from the doorway to the lounge.

"Ashley!" everyone called, happy to see her.

Phoebe came up and gave her a hug. "I'm glad you're here," she said. "I'm really sorry you didn't get chosen for the panel. You're such a good writer – you really deserved to be on it."

"Thanks," Ashley said.

"Make a spot on the floor," Phoebe said to everyone. "We need more room."

Mary-Kate scooted over so that Ashley and Phoebe could put their sleeping bags next to each other. Then everyone grabbed a piece of pizza.

"You know what the worst part of today was?" Ashley said.

"What?" Phoebe asked.

"Being dressed like Mrs. Langstrom!" Ashley said, laughing. "It was really creepy."

"Hey – it's not your problem," Samantha said. "It's hers. She was probably trying to look young and hip. My mom is always doing that. She thinks she's a teenager or something."

"I don't know," Ashley said. "Maybe. But after that, I felt like I needed a makeover!"

"You?" Wendy cried. "Are you crazy? You have the best total fashion sense of anyone I know! Me, on the other hand – I'd pay a fortune for a fashion makeover."

Campbell dropped her pizza on to a paper plate. "That's it, Mary-Kate!" she cried. "That's how you can make the money to buy your snowboard!"

Huh? Mary-Kate was confused. "How?" she asked.

"You can hold a raffle!" Campbell cried. "Sell tickets and have a draw. And the winner gets a makeover from Ashley!"

"Lots of girls would want a makeover from the Fashion Editor of the *Acorn*!" Cheryl said.

A raffle? Mary-Kate thought. It sounded like a good idea. But it was too late. The snowboard was going back on the floor tomorrow. She could never pull off a raffle in time. And besides . . .

"I have a better idea," Mary-Kate announced, her eyes dancing. "A much better idea!"

CHAPTER THIRTEEN

"This is the best idea I've had all year!" Mary-Kate announced. She sat up on her knees so she could explain it to everyone. "Campbell's right – we should have a raffle. And the prize would be a makeover. But not so I can buy a snowboard. So we can buy a microwave!"

"That's brilliant!" Elise chimed in.

The other girls looked excited, too.

"That would be awesome!" Ashley said. "But hello . . . are you really my sister? I mean, I thought you wanted a snowboard so badly, you'd do anything to get it."

"Anything? Would that include eating her own jumble-crumble bars?" Campbell joked.

Mary-Kate laughed and shook her head. "Look, I do want a snowboard – desperately," she said. "But it's too late for the Powder Pounder. I need the money by tomorrow – and there's no way that's going to happen. Besides, you can't just hold a raffle for yourself."

"Why not?" Campbell said.

"I think it's illegal or something," Mary-Kate said. "I think raffles are only for charity."

And besides that, Mary-Kate thought, *it would feel good to do something for everyone else.*

"Way cool," Phoebe said. "I love this idea. I'll make the posters!"

"Hold it," Wendy said. "First Ashley has to agree to do the makeover."

"No problem!" Ashley said quickly. "You know me – I'm always ready to give out fashion advice. Unless you think maybe Phoebe should do the makeover. She's a fashion editor for the *Acorn*, too."

"No!" Wendy blurted out. All the other girls shook their heads.

"Sorry, Phoebe," Samantha explained. "You know we love you – but you're the only person who can pull off that vintage style. The rest of us need normal fashion help!"

"Okay, so I'll do the makeover," Ashley said. She

smiled for the first time that night.

This is going to be so much fun! Mary-Kate thought. She jumped up. She couldn't wait to get started on the project.

"I'll go get permission from Miss Viola," she told her friends.

Mary-Kate knocked on Miss Viola's door and explained the plan.

"A raffle? To buy a new microwave for the dorm?" Miss Viola thought about it for a minute. "I don't see why not," she said finally.

"Thanks!" Mary-Kate hurried back to the lounge.

For the next few hours, the girls worked on the raffle. Wendy made tickets. Phoebe and Ashley made posters. And Mary-Kate and Campbell made flyers to hand out in class.

By three in the morning, Mary-Kate was so tired she thought she'd fall over. She dragged herself to the bathroom to brush her teeth.

Ashley and Campbell were already there, getting ready for bed.

"Good party," Ashley said to Mary-Kate.

"Yeah," Mary-Kate said with a yawn. "It almost makes up for not getting my snowboard."

"But at least you've come up with one moneymaking idea that's really going to work,"

Ashley said, trying to cheer her up. "And we'll have a microwave in the dorm when you're through!"

"Ashley? Wake up! Wake up!" a voice said.

Wake up? Ashley thought. *I just fell asleep a few hours ago!*

She glanced at the clock on the lounge wall. It was only ten on Saturday morning. She and her friends had stayed up really late, talking about the raffle. Now her back was sore from sleeping on the floor all night.

"Ashley, you have a phone call," Wendy said, shaking her again.

A phone call? At this hour? Ashley thought. *How weird.*

"Who is it?" Ashley mumbled.

"It's an adult," Wendy said. "Miss Viola answered the phone in the hall, and she says some woman is asking for you."

Ashley rubbed her eyes and dragged herself to her feet.

"Okay," she said, yawning. She stumbled to the phone. "Hello?"

"Hello, Ashley?" the woman on the other end of the line said. "This is Andrea Langstrom, Peaches' mother."

82

CHAPTER FOURTEEN

"Let's hear it for my twin sister, the brilliant mastermind of the First Annual Porter House Makeover Raffle – Mary-Kate Burke!" Ashley announced through a microphone.

"Yay!" Everyone in the student U cheered and applauded.

The big room of the student U was packed with girls. Most of them were first- and second-formers. They had all bought tickets for the makeover raffle.

Ashley stood on a chair, holding a microphone. The new microwave oven they had bought with the raffle money sat on a table nearby.

"And three cheers for the new Porter House microwave!" Ashley exclaimed. "Popcorn is on the house, thanks to all the Porter House girls!"

Everyone cheered as Wendy passed out bowls of hot popcorn.

"And before we hold the draw," Ashley went on, "we have to give a big shout-out to all the people who worked so hard to make this raffle a success. So let's hear it for Phoebe, who made some awesome posters . . . "

Everyone cheered again.

"And a big way-to-go to Campbell Smith and Mary-Kate, who made the tickets . . . " Ashley continued.

More cheers and applause.

"And we couldn't have done it without Wendy, Samantha, Elise, and Cheryl, who sold tickets all week," Ashley added. Everyone clapped less this time. Ashley knew it was because they wanted her to get on with the draw.

"Okay, okay, it's time to draw the winning ticket!" Ashley announced.

Everyone fell silent and Ashley looked at Mary-Kate. Mary-Kate was supposed to come up and hold the goldfish bowl that was full of ticket stubs.

But Mary-Kate was staring out of the window.

It was snowing!

No wonder Mary-Kate isn't paying attention, Ashley

thought. *I bet she's thinking about the big ski trip the team will be going on next week.*

"And now for the winner," Ashley said to get Mary-Kate's attention.

Mary-Kate snapped out of it. She climbed up on to another chair and held the fish bowl for Ashley.

Everyone got really quiet.

Mary-Kate reached in and stirred the tickets with her hand. Then Ashley closed her eyes and picked one out.

"And the winner is . . . Sarah Inglenook!" Ashley announced.

Sarah was a second-form girl with long curly red hair. She jumped up and down. "Yes!" she screamed as she pushed forwards through the crowd. "I won the makeover! Can we get started right away?"

Everyone laughed and Sarah's friends congratulated her.

Then the girls who hadn't won went back to talking and playing video games or left the student U. A bunch of Porter House girls came up to thank Mary-Kate again for helping them get the microwave.

"I'm serious," Sarah repeated when the crowd had thinned out. "Can we start on my makeover now?"

"Well, sure – why not?" Ashley answered.

"Great!" Sarah said.

Ashley and Mary-Kate grabbed their coats and followed Sarah to her dorm. She lived in Hambrook House, a stone building near a big cluster of trees.

"That was so great," Ashley said to Mary-Kate as the two of them walked across the campus. "Everyone is so happy about the microwave. And it's all because of you!"

"Thanks," Mary-Kate said proudly. "Yeah, I'm really glad we did it. That felt good."

"But you still feel bad about not getting your snowboard, don't you?" Ashley asked softly as they climbed the stairs to Sarah's room.

Mary-Kate shrugged. "It's okay."

That's a lie, Ashley thought. *I can tell she really feels bad about it.*

"I mean, I wanted a snowboard a lot," Mary-Kate admitted. "And it's a bummer that I can't be on the team this year. But I talked to Dad last night, and he said maybe I can be on the team next year. Anyway, I'm glad we got the microwave for Porter House."

"Did you say snowboard?" Sarah asked, turning around as she unlocked her dorm room. "Because I have a snowboard I never want to see again."

Ashley's eyes popped open wide. "You do?" she said.

There, leaning in the corner of Sarah's room, was a beautiful orange-and-white snowboard. Brand-new.

Mary-Kate's mouth fell open. "Wow!" she said, staring at it. "It's even better than the Powder Pounder!"

"My dad brought it for me when he came to visit last week," Sarah said. "He wants me to be into sports – and it was on sale or something. But I wouldn't go down a mountain if you paid me! You can use it any time you want, Mary-Kate."

"Are you kidding?" Mary-Kate screamed. "That's fantastic!"

She ran over and gave Sarah a hug.

"No problem," Sarah said. "Keep it in your room if you want."

"I don't believe this!" Mary-Kate cried. "This is the best surprise! I'll have to do something to thank you."

"Uh-oh," Ashley said. "Like what? Watch out, Sarah – and be very afraid if it involves baking or ironing."

Mary-Kate laughed. "Don't worry," she said to Sarah. "I'll get Ashley to bake you a batch of her famous jumble-crumble bars as a thank-you."

Oh, no, Ashley thought. *Here we go again!*

ACORN

The Voice of White Oak Academy Since 1905

FROSTY ROCKS!
by Elise Van Hook

Who says White Oak is an all-girls school? You can't prove it by strolling across the campus these days — because the walkways are covered with men. *Snow* men!

That's right — last weekend the snow fell like crazy, so Mrs. Pritchard declared a spur-of-the-moment snowman-building contest!

The girls from each dorm joined together to create a snowman fashion show. Phipps went for the sporty look. They dressed their snowman in ski poles and goggles.

Porter House went for the traditional look. Their snowman donned a top hat, cane, and red scarf.

But the big winner was Marble Manor. Their snowman was punked out! He had short, spiky hair, an earring – and he was holding a cardboard guitar! Talk about a totally *cool* dude!

Yesterday at breakfast the girls of Marble Manor were given a prize for their rockin' snowman that's sure to keep their toes toasty: a month's supply of flavoured oatmeal!

IT'S ALL DOWNHILL FROM HERE!
by Mary-Kate Burke

Sports pro Mary-Kate Burke

Grab your snowboards, strap on your ski boots, and get ready to hit the slopes! For the first season ever, White Oak has its very own winter sports team – and all you have to do to make the team is sign up!

That's right – thanks to Coach Franklin, even beginners are welcome to join. Coach will teach the newbie skiers how to swish and snowplow their way downhill. Or, if you're snowboarding, maybe he'll teach you how to not fall down!

So come on, snow bunnies, let's boogie! But be forewarned: you may be spending a lot of time on your backside! The first trip to the mountain is scheduled in just a few weeks. Let it snow, let it snow, let it snow!

THE GET-REAL GIRL

Dear Get-Real Girl,
The guy I like is so cute, so funny, so smart – and so taken! He's going out with my best friend, but I can't stop drooling over him! Is it okay to go after him? All's fair in love and war – right?
Signed,
Smitten

Dear Smitten,
Going after your best friend's honey is No-No

SMITTEN MITTEN

Number One. And don't kid yourself with that "all's fair in love and war" stuff either – unless you're ready for battle! Because if you try to steal your best friend's boy, she is *not* going to be happy.

Just remember: your best friend is so much more important to you than this guy will ever be. So keep your smitten mittens off!
Signed,
Get-Real Girl

Dear Get-Real Girl,
My roomie borrowed my best cashmere sweater. When she returned it, there was a big hot-fudge stain on the front. She says the stain was there when I loaned it to her, but I say no way. Who should pay for the dry cleaning?
Signed,
Sticky Situation

Dear Sticky Situation,
Your roomie claims that she borrowed a sweater that had a big hot-fudge stain on the front and *wore* it that way? And what did she wear it with – maraschino cherry earrings?

Tell your roomie it's time to get real. She should obviously chip in for the dry cleaning. But just to keep the peace, why don't you pay for half the bill? After all, you were going to clean it eventually anyway – we hope!

Signed,
Get-Real Girl

THE FIRST FORM BUZZ

by Dana Woletsky

The weather report must be all messed up these days. The forecast calls for snow – even though the gossip at White Oak is hot enough to melt a glacier!

First up, the hottest rumours on campus are all about MKB – again! The story is that she got burned trying to bake and sell some very strange

cookies. You know what they say, MK: if you can't take the heat, get out of the kitchen!

While we're talking about food follies, did anyone notice DH accidentally dump her dinner on her shirt last night? Seriously, DH – maybe you ought to try accessorizing that shirt next time – with a bib!

And speaking of bibs, guess who else needs one? A certain AB has been *drooling* over the chance to be on the teen panel for *Cool It* magazine. But let's face it, AB – my sources agree you're not cool enough for the job!

That's it for the buzz. Remember my motto: if you want the scoop, you just gotta snoop!

GLAM GAB
by Ashley Burke and
Phoebe Cahill

Fashion expert Ashley Burke

Quick – name the coolest magazine on the planet!

If you said *Cool It*, you're so right! Everyone at White Oak agrees that *Cool It* is the best place to get fashion advice and check out the newest looks for teens.

But guess what makes *Cool It* twice as cool these days? The fact that the editor of the magazine is Andrea Langstrom – the mother of White Oak's very own Langstrom sisters, Julia and Heather!

Mrs. Langstrom will be the special guest at our morning announcements on Friday. She'll be unveiling the names of five White Oak girls who will be featured in the magazine next month!

That's right – five White Oak students will be part of a new teen panel for *Cool It*. These five lucky girls will lend their fashion advice to teens all over the country. And guess who tried out? Ours truly!

So good luck to all the con-

testants. And even if you don't make it – we think you're 2 cool 2 B 4-gotten!

UPCOMING CALENDAR
Fall / Winter

Calling all pumpkin artists! It's time to cut loose and carve out a name for yourself at the annual Pumpkin Carving Contest! Prizes will be awarded to the most original designs. Can you dig it?

Can't go home for the holidays? No problem! You can spend winter break at Harrington. (Don't worry – the guys have to clean out their

rooms before the girls move in!) To find out more, come to the Harrington for the Holidays meeting on Monday at 6:00 in the Student U.

Let's talk turkey – and cranberries, and stuffing, too! Thanksgiving is just around the corner, so let's all chip in for the canned food drive to help homeless families. You can make a difference!

Lost and found in the dining hall: a gazillion gloves, hats, scarves, and mittens. So if you're spending your days with one hand freezing in the cold because you don't know where that glove is, check out the lost and found! You just might find the perfect match.

IT'S ALL IN THE STARS
Fall Horoscopes

Leo
(July 22-August 21)

They say it's a jungle out there. But does that stop you, Leo? Not this month! You're the leader of the pack, so when you roar — your friends listen!

Just remember that even the best leaders know how to follow other people every once in a while. By standing back and letting someone else have her say, you might learn a new way to solve a problem.

Virgo
(August 22-September 22)

You're usually a down-to-earth sign, but this month you should reach for the stars! Your life will shine this month, Virgo. Now is the time to go after what you've been dreaming about lately. If you're dying to try a new hobby, do it! If you've been too shy in the past to talk to that special guy, now is your chance!

Libra
(September 23-October 22)

Everyone says you're the very best kind of friend: loyal, fair-minded, and kind. You never want to hurt anyone's feelings — which is one reason why people love to hang around you. But this month, don't be afraid to speak up and say what's on your mind. You just might be surprised at the results!

PSST! Take a sneak peek
at

Sealed With A Kiss

"I am not going through that door," Ashley said, crossing her arms.

"Come on, Ashley!" Mary-Kate nudged her sister. "It's not every day you find an underground tunnel leading to Harrington."

"It's too dark to see where we're going," Ashley complained. "There could be mice or spiderwebs or something in there!"

"Leave it to me," Elise said. She pulled a shiny object out of her pocket. "This Day-Glo glitter gloss is bright enough to light up any room." She handed the tube to Mary-Kate.

"Excellent!" Mary-Kate exclaimed. "Forward march, troops. We're out to explore new territory!"

Mary-Kate led the girls down the hallway. She held the tube of glitter gloss in front of her like a lantern. But pretty soon the girls didn't need the gloss any more. The tunnel got lighter and lighter.

"Look," Mary-Kate said, pointing ahead. The tunnel suddenly ended – and opened up into a huge room.

"Whoa, check it out," Cheryl said, sounding awed. The room was packed with sports posters and video games.

"Girls," Kristen said, rubbing her hands together, "I think we're in serious boy country!"

"How did all this stuff get here?" Ashley asked, picking up a book from the floor.

Mary-Kate opened her mouth to answer but was interrupted by a door creaking behind them.

She turned around slowly. A shadow appeared from behind the door.

"Wh-what's that?" Elise stammered.

"It's a ghost," Kristen whispered.

"Or a giant mouse!" Ashley shrieked, jumping behind Mary-Kate.

But it wasn't a ghost or a giant mouse. The mysterious shadow turned out to be a boy. And he was the cutest boy Mary-Kate had ever seen!

mary-kateandashley
TWO of a kind ™

 HarperCollins*Entertainment*

 PARACHUTE PRESS

 DUALSTAR PUBLICATIONS

 mary-kateandashley.com
AOL Keyword: mary-kateandashley

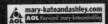

Join Mary-Kate and Ashley as they unleash a hurricane of action and romance

Coming to video
and DVD
February 2003*

date correct at time of going to press

It's
What
YOU
Watch.

Distributed by

mary-kateandashley

Sweet 16

(1) *Never Been Kissed*   (0 00 714879 8)
(2) *Wishes and Dreams*   (0 00 714880 1)
(3) *The Perfect Summer*   (0 00 714881 X)

HarperCollins*Entertainment*

PARACHUTE PRESS

DUALSTAR PUBLICATIONS

mary-kateandashley.com
AOL Keyword: mary-kateandashley

the mary-kateandashley brand

brand

Fab freebies!

You can have loads of fun with these ultra-cool Glistening Stix from the **mary-kateandashley** brand. Great glam looks for eyes, lips – or anywhere else you fancy!

All you have to do is **collect four tokens from four different books from the mary-kateandashley** brand (no photocopies, please!), send them to us with your address on the coupon below – and a groovy Glistening Stix will be on its way to you!

Go on, get collecting and sparkle like a star!

Real Books for Real Girls

It's What YOU Read

TOKEN

Name: ....

Address: ....

....

e-mail: ....

☐ Tick here if you do not wish to receive further information about children's books.

Send coupon to: **mary-kateandashley Marketing**,
HarperCollins Publishers, 77-85 Fulham Palace Road, Hammersmith, London W6 8JB.

Terms and conditions: proof of sending cannot be considered proof of receipt. Not redeemable for cash. 28 days delivery. Offer open to UK residents only. **Photocopies not accepted.**